DEBORA VOGRIG is a high school literature teacher and the author of *Line and Scribble* (Chronicle). She lives in Italy.

PIA VALENTINIS is the illustrator of *Line and Scribble* (Chronicle), *The Garden of Monsieur Monet* (Royal Academy), and many other books for children and adults. She was awarded the XXI Italian Andersen Prize for Best Illustrator, and her books have been published in over a dozen countries. Pia lives in Italy. Visit her website at piavalentinis.com.

For Clelia, Lidia, Alfredo, and the other inhabitants of Via Pirano.

– Debora and Pia

Text © 2021 Debora Vogrig • Illustrations © 2021 Pia Valentinis
Book design by Orith Kolodny
Published by arrangement with Debbie Bibo Agency

First published in the United States in 2021
by Eerdmans Books for Young Readers, an imprint of Wm. B. Eerdmans Publishing Co.
Grand Rapids, Michigan • www.eerdmans.com/youngreaders

29 28 27 26 25 24 23 22 21   1 2 3 4 5 6 7 8 9

Library of Congress Cataloging-in-Publication Data

Names: Vogrig, Debora, author. | Valentinis, Pia, illustrator.
Title: Black and White / Debora Vogrig ; [illustrated by] Pia Valentinis.
Description: Grand Rapids, Michigan : Eerdmans Books for Young Readers,
   2022. | Audience: Ages 4-8. | Summary: "Black and White are very
   different. But when they work together, the two colors can go on the
   most amazing adventures"— Provided by publisher.
Identifiers: LCCN 2021000052 | ISBN 9780802855756 (hardcover)
Subjects: CYAC: Black—Fiction. | White—Fiction. | Color—Fiction. |
   Friendship—Fiction.
Classification: LCC PZ7.1.V66 Bl 2022 | DDC [E]--dc23
LC record available at https://lccn.loc.gov/2021000052

Illustrations created with pen and digital materials

DEBORA VOGRIG | PIA VALENTINIS

Black and White

EERDMANS BOOKS FOR YOUNG READERS

GRAND RAPIDS, MICHIGAN

White wakes up . . .

. . . and spreads through the sky.

But when White goes through the window . . .

. . . Black hides under the bed.

"Hey, Black!"
says White.
"Where are you?"

"There you are!"
says White.

"Hey, stop pushing,"
grumbles Black.
"You're squashing me!"

"Oh, all right, I'm going,"
says White.

"No, wait!" yells Black.
"Don't go! I want to
show you something!"

"What?" asks White, running off.

"This!"
replies Black,
spraying something.

"Stop it!"
screams White.
"Look what you've done!"

"Wow! Check this out!"
says Black.
"So cool!"

"Friends?"
asks White.

"Friends!"
replies Black.

So Black and White delve into the forest together . . .

. . . and take a journey from the North Pole

to the South Pole.

They gallop through the savanna . . .

. . . and lie in wait in the jungle.

Now, let the winds blow!

"Ahoy! Full speed ahead!"
Black and White holler together.

Then Black descends on the houses

and stretches out everything . . .

Abracadabra!

Just one more game!

Just one more page, and then . . .

"Good night, White,"
says Black.

"Good night, Black,"
says White.